The Berenstain

Pet Rescue

Let's give our
animal friends a break.
Adopt one now,
for goodness' sake!

Mike Berenstain

Based on the characters created by
Stan and Jan Berenstain

HARPER FESTIVAL
An Imprint of HarperCollins Publishers

Library of Congress Control Number: 2018939987 ISBN 978-0-06-265464-9
Typography by Honee Jang
20 21 22 CWM 10 9 8 7 6 5 4   ❖ First Edition

There was a special assembly going on at the Bear Country School, deep in Bear Country. Volunteers from the local animal shelter were visiting with a group of pets. All the cubs at school were excited to meet and learn about these new animal friends.

"Hello, everyone!" said a volunteer. "I'm Patty from the Bear Country Animal Shelter. I'm here to introduce you to some special guests. They are all what we call 'rescue pets.' These animals have been taken from places where they were not treated well. They need special care to get better before they can be adopted by new families."

Would any of you cubs like to come up on stage and meet our pets?" asked Patty.

Of course, all the students raised their hands. Brother, Sister, and Cousin Fred were picked. They got to pet a dog named Lucky and a cat named Purrcival.

Then a parrot named Mac perched on Sister's shoulder while Brother held a hamster named Fluff. Cousin Fred put out his finger and a colorful lizard named Zippy climbed onto his hand.

"All of these pets and many more are up for adoption at the animal shelter," Patty told them. "Please come and visit us. Maybe you could give a good home to one of these wonderful animals."

After school, Brother, Sister, and Fred walked home together.

"It would be nice to adopt one of those pets," said Sister.

"Yes," agreed Brother, "but we already have several pets. That's probably enough for us."

"As a matter of fact," said Fred, "I am going to adopt a pet from the animal shelter. I've been visiting a lot and have one picked out. I'm going there right after school to bring it home."

"Wow!" said Brother and Sister. "Can we come with you?"

"Sure!" said Fred.

Everything was arranged with Mama and Papa. Fred's parents picked the cubs up and they headed for the animal shelter. As they arrived, Patty met them at the door.

"So glad you all could come!" she said. "Let's start with a tour of the shelter."

Patty showed them around. There was a big room where volunteers were caring for pets—grooming them, petting them, snuggling with them, and playing with them.

"It's good for pets who have been treated badly to get comfortable with people in this way. When the animals first come to us they can be very shy and fearful. But with patience and kindness, most begin to feel safe and happy."

Hi! My name is Ollie

Hi! My name is Scruff

About me:

Hi! My name is Penny

About me:

I've been Adopted!

Hi! My name is Speck

About me:

Patty moved on to the areas where the pets lived. The dogs and cats were kept in nice bright pens where they had plenty of food and water.

The smaller animals like hamsters, guinea pigs, birds, and lizards were cared for in pleasant cages where they had plenty of toys and places to exercise.

"Now Fred," said Patty, "let's get together with your own special rescue pet."

Patty brought out Taffy—a cute, caramel-colored little dog.

Taffy came right up to Fred, wagging her tail and licking his hand. Fred had met and played with Taffy many times before.

At first, Taffy was shy with Brother and Sister. She hid behind Fred. But after a while, she felt more confident. She sniffed their hands, wagged her tail, and let them pet her.

"Taffy has come a long way!" said Patty. "When she first came to us, she was afraid of all strangers. But after she met Fred and got to know and trust him, she's become much more confident."

SQUEAK!

"Well, Fred," said Patty, "this is the big moment. The adoption paperwork is all done—are you ready to take Taffy home?"

"Yes!" said Fred, very excited. "I sure am—I can hardly wait!"

So with Taffy on a leash, Fred led her outside to the car. At first, she was worried about getting in the car. But Fred was very patient, petting and soothing her.

Finally, she felt more secure and climbed in with Fred.

When they arrived at Fred's house, they led Taffy inside and let her explore her new home. She was very curious and sniffed and poked into every nook and cranny.

Then they took Taffy outside to explore the yard. The yard was surrounded by a strong fence to keep Taffy safe inside. Taffy loved the yard. She sniffed in the flower beds and scratched in the nice soft earth.

She saw some birds and a squirrel. She happily ran after them, barking loudly. The birds flew off and the squirrel dashed up a tree where it chittered angrily, waving its tail at the annoying dog. Taffy was very happy!

Fred took out a Frisbee and tossed it across the yard. Delighted, Taffy chased after it, grabbed it, and ran back to Fred, laying it at his feet.

Brother and Sister took turns tossing the Frisbee to Taffy. She ran back and forth across the yard until they were all tired out. She sat down in a heap, panting happily.

The cubs gathered around their new friend and gave her a big group bear hug. They loved their new rescue pet. It felt so good to know that she now had a safe and loving home!